TOTO

THE NINJA CAT

AND THE INCREDIBLE CHEESE HEIST

DERMOT O'LEARY

ILLUSTRATED BY NICK EAST

HODDER CHILDREN'S BOOKS

First published in Great Britain in 2018 by Hodder and Stoughton

1 3 5 7 9 10 8 6 4 2

Text copyright © Dermot O'Leary, 2018
Illustrations copyright © Nick East, 2018
Inside back cover photograph by Ray Burmiston

ISBN 978 1 444 93947 7

Printed and bound in Great Britain by Clays Ltd, Elcograf S.p.A
The paper and board used in this book are made from wood from
responsible sources

Hodder Children's Books
An imprint of Hachette Children's Group
Part of Hodder and Stoughton
Carmelite House
50 Victoria Embankment
London EC4Y 0DZ
An Hachette UK Company
www.hachette.co.uk
www.hachettechildrens.co.uk

TO DEE KOPPANG O'LEARY,

first of her name,

Queen of the Fjords,

proud woman of Kent,

and most definitely Mother of Cats.

CHAPTER 1

'OK, Silver,' the bushy-tailed cat said to himself, 'empty your mind, you can do this. Don't worry about the last twenty-four attempts.'

'Let's go over it again,' said his sister Toto, with a smile.

'You leap, then bounce off the glass window to the left, off the wall to the right, then dive for the handle and hey presto, we've got an open fridge!'

'And just to be clear, this is all with my eyes shut?' Silver asked.

'You said you wanted to do some ninja training,' laughed Toto. 'The *Double-wall-bounce-open-fridge* is one of the first moves you learn. Except, well, I may have added the "open-fridge" bit ...'

Silver looked up at the fridge, he really did want to eat. Their human Mamma and Papa were out, and they'd finished their cat food hours ago. He knew he could never be an **ACTUAL NINJA**, like his sister – that would take ages and lots of practice and training, and he was far too impatient and **HUNGRY** for all of that. But a couple of moves would be really cool. Plus it wouldn't hurt his reputation with the neighbourhood cats. Especially that lovely ginger (*que bella!*) who'd moved in across the street and who he quite fancied – not that he'd ever admit that to his sister ... there'd be no living it down.

'You can do this, Silver,' he muttered to himself. He took a running jump, launched

BOSH!

WHOOOOOSH

BOP!

himself at the window – so far so good – and then bounced onto the wall ...

This is it, he thought as he hurtled through the air, *I'm going to make it, my first Ninja move!*

'**HERE WE GOOO ... ARGH ...** '

Silver opened his eyes and realised his leap from the wall wasn't far enough. He was about to miss the fridge and crash into the freezer door below for the twenty-fifth painful time. He closed his eyes again and braced for impact ... but incredibly, none came. Instead he felt a **WHOOSH** of wind in his whiskers as his sister grabbed him, and pulled him to safety on the kitchen counter. Somehow (and very coolly) opening the fridge on her way past!

'I almost had it sis, almost. But thanks for stopping my poor nose from getting another bashing.'

'No sweat,' replied Toto, 'you'll get it one day. I just couldn't hear you crash land again, no matter how funny it is. And let me tell you bro, it doesn't get any less funny.'

'Knock it off,' replied Silver, giving her a friendly nip on the ear, 'it's not easy being the famous *TOTO THE NINJA CAT'S BROTHER*.'

He was right, Toto was practically famous these days ... well, at least on their street. All their animal neighbours were very impressed and grateful that she had captured a terrifying King Cobra known as Brian and returned him to the zoo. Now, they couldn't stop themselves from giving her high-paws whenever they bumped into her. (Although truth be told, Brian was actually a really nice guy who was just trying to save his girlfriend Brenda from illegal pet traders, which Toto and Silver were only too happy to help him with ...)

It had been an amazing first adventure which had happened right after the kittens moved to London from Italy. The escapade had also involved meeting **CATFACE** (a rat who lives his life as a cat – it's complicated, but it works for everyone), who had become their new best friend and guide to their new home.

As much as she enjoyed her status, Toto knew that she wouldn't have been able to do any of it without Silver. Toto was almost completely blind, and could only see light and dark shapes. Silver acted as her eyes and, as far as she was concerned, they came as a team.

Since that adventure, their lives had been very quiet, without much need for ninja skills. Even though she was highly trained, Toto hadn't been given her first mission yet. In fact, the group of ninjas she belonged to, the **ANCIENT ORDER OF INTERNATIONAL NINJA CATS**, was so secret that apart from her old Italian sensei Ventura, she didn't even know who any of the other members were! So, Toto had been trying to teach Silver her best moves to make sure she didn't get out of practice …

Toto jumped gently from the counter top to the fridge and began rooting around.

'So, what are we going to eat?' she asked,

her big black furry tail flicking back and forth as she used her sense of smell to guide her. 'Mmmm … what have we got … I can smell loads. Chicken, salami, sardines, your favourite strawberry yoghurt*, leftover roast beef, carrots **(YUCK!)**, half a sausage,

* Silver is obsessed with dairy. Just in case you ever want to buy him a present.

and my favourite ... **CHEESE** ... no, wait a second, I **CAN'T** smell cheese ... I'm sure they bought some yesterday. Why can't I smell it?'

'There's a very good reason for that sis – it's not there! It looks like all the cheese has gone, every single crumb!'

CHAPTER 2

'How can there possibly be no cheese?'
THERE'S ALWAYS CHEESE,' said Toto,
scratching her head as they made their way
through the cat flap into the garden.

It was a glorious, sunny day in Camden,
and there wasn't a cat in London who
wouldn't be taking the rare opportunity to
bask in the heat. The two kittens headed
to the lawn for a roll on the grass and a

nice spot of grooming.

'Beats me,' replied Silver between licks of his shiny coat. 'It doesn't make any sense. I was looking forward to some cheese for lunch; a nice bit of gorgonzola, or even some ricotta, **_MAMMA MIA_**.' He licked his lips and rolled over on his back as if in a cheesey dream world of his own. 'Be honest sis, did you take it? I know you love a midnight snack.'

'No, **_I DID NOT_**,' said Toto. 'I mean, I was tempted, but you know we're a team – I wouldn't do that to you.'

'Well, someone's taken the cheese, and it's not Mamma and Papa – I watch them like a hawk. Any time they're by the fridge, I'm at their feet like one of those stupid dogs that live down the street, tongue out, on hind legs looking cute, begging for scraps – works every time. Suckers! You should try it— *TOTO! STOP!!! TOTO!* What are you doing?'

Abandoning her sunbathing, Silver's near-blind sister had leaped into the air after a flash of green feathers. Two and half somersaults later and the the poor unfortunate bird was pinned to the floor.

'Toto!' cried Silver. 'That's Robert the Parakeet, he's our friend. What on earth do you think you're playing at?'

'He's right,' squawked Robert. 'Remember me? I live around the corner in Regents Park in a lovely Japanese elm. I have two kids and a wife called Judith. I warned you about

Brian's escape last year. I'm your neighbour – I know Catface! **PLEASE DON'T TEAR MY FEATHERS** ... I spent ages fluffing them this morning ... can you let me go ... please?'

'I am **SO SORRY**,' said Toto, climbing off the poor ruffled bird. 'I don't know what came over me. We were talking about a cheese thief having raided our fridge when I saw the break in light as you flew over, and I'm afraid the ninja training kicked in. Are you OK?'

'It's not the friendliest welcome I've ever had, but no harm done I suppose,' replied the flustered parakeet.

'Can we get you anything?' asked Silver, trying to repair some of the damage. 'Mamma and Papa have some sunflower seeds in the birdfeeder, and I can fetch you some water too.'

The parakeet perked up a bit when he heard the mention of food. He plonked himself down on the grass as Silver, ever the charmer, brought everything over.

'I have to say, this is a lovely spread, quite makes up for, you know, almost being torn to shreds,' Robert said as he tucked into his impromptu picnic.

Toto looked sheepish, and shrugged her

shoulders. 'Sorry, you can't exactly turn off being a ninja. How have you been, anyway?'

'Oh, I'm all right. Summer is always the best time to be a parakeet in London. School holidays are in full swing, so the city empties out, it's a lovely time to fly. We're the messengers for all the animals of London you see – well, us and the pigeons, but we're a lot faster. So, if animals need to send urgent letters they call us. I'm a manager now, got a promotion recently.'

'*CONGRATULATIONS!*' chimed the cats in unison.

'Thanks so much, my family are ever so proud. Which brings me to why I'm here: I've got delivery for you,' he said getting an envelope out of his bag.

The cats looked at each other, and could barely contain their excitement – they'd never had a delivery before. Who was it from? What was it? They were dying to find out.

'Is it cheese?' asked Silver, hopefully.

'Does it look like cheese?' Robert replied looking at Silver like he'd gone mad. 'Of course it's not cheese! For the heavy-duty deliveries we use wood pigeons – those guys can carry some weight. No – it's a letter addressed to Toto. Well, I'd best be off. Thanks for the grub, try not to ambush me next time ... I think I might use the doorbell,

The cats had loved travelling on the tube the first time they'd used it with Catface, but the vibe now was totally different.

'Why does everyone look so grumpy?' Silver asked Toto as they descended the spiral staircase into the beautiful ticket hall, with its black and white tiles and sparkling chandeliers.

The cats got into the queue at the ticket counter.

'NEXT!' cried an impatient voice from behind the ticket booth.

'Oh, hi,' said Silver, 'we need to get to Downing Street.' He handed their oyster shells over to the ticket-master, a Persian cat. Whilst humans travel on the tube with oyster cards, the animals of London use actual oyster shells – far nicer looking and a lot tastier to make!

'Not another fool with no idea how to use their oyster shell? As if I haven't got enough to do, for kitty's sake ... are you two tourists? I can tell from your accents and that terrible hat,' the rude ticket-master moaned.

'Firstly, we are **NOT** tourists, we're Londoners, and even if we were, you are not setting a very good example of hospitality!' said Toto. 'Secondly, we simply need a little guidance, which I'd have thought is your job ... and thirdly ... *MY BROTHER LOOKS VERY COOL IN HIS HAT!*'

'All right, keep your hair on. I'm sorry, it's just that I haven't had any lunch, and I'm a little "h-angry". Ran out of cheese you see, and I was really looking forward to that cheese and pickle sandwich ... Strangest thing, thought I had loads of lovely cheddar in the fridge. Anyway, you'll want

Westminster station. I've topped these oysters up – just put your shell over the sensor and the gates will open ...' He took a quick breath then screamed '**NEXT!**', his mood obviously not brightened by remembering his missing lunch.

As the cats made their way to the train, they could sense everyone, be they dogs or birds, ferrets or hedgehogs, was in a foul mood.

'Seriously, what is it with these guys?' Silver asked Toto.

'Never mind them, we've got bigger fish to fry. Hold on tight, Silver.'

The train picked up speed as it left the station. And no matter how grumpy they might have been, all the animals on board were grateful for the rush of wind to cool the summer heat on the platform.

CHAPTER 4

'Toto, thank goodness you're here. Quickly, come inside.'

Even though he looked his usual well-groomed self, dressed in an impeccable grey suit and bowler hat, it was clear that Larry was far from relaxed as he opened the grand wooden cat flap at the side of 10 Downing Street and ushered his guests in.

The kittens had made their way easily

enough from the tube at Westminster, but Toto had to agree with Silver – everyone on the way had looked a bit surly and glum. Even with her limited eyesight she was getting the impression that the whole of London was in a **BAD** mood. The police officers looked bored and distracted, the cab drivers were honking their horns even more than usual, and the school children they'd passed looked like they might be about to throw tantrums, and end up on the naughty step. And now the worry etched on Larry's face made it even more evident: something was up.

They followed Larry, padding their way down a short hall into a small, dark, wooden lift (known in the human world

as a dumb waiter, the kind you sometimes
see in restaurants to move food between
floors). It could just about fit all three cats
in. Larry pulled the old iron shutters closed
and pushed a button. The lift descended
deep into the building, and when it came
to a stop they stepped out into in an

underground office. In the centre, there was an old wooden desk, covered in papers and lit by a green desk light. Facing it were two very nappable-looking leather armchairs and, to the side, a drinks trolley with five or six different types of milk in beautiful crystal decanters.

What was most striking about the office, though, were the pictures on the walls. Each one was a portrait painting of a different cat. There was one who looked Victorian, another in military uniform from the First World War. There were many wearing monocles or top hats, there were some in full regimental dress, and others wore fancy suits. They all looked proud and very, **VERY** important.

'My predecessors,' explained Larry, after Silver had quietly described the scene to his sister. 'But before I tell you about them, where are my manners? This might be a crisis, but there's no room for rudeness. Toto, Silver, what can I get you to drink? Let me see I've got some organic, some ordinary semi-skimmed, almond for those of you

who might be allergic to dairy (at this Silver looked very confused). No, I think we need something stronger. How about a couple of glasses of **JERSEY MILK?** Yes, that's the stuff.'

He licked his lips as he expertly poured the creamy milk into Martini glasses. Toto sipped hers slowly – it was like nothing she'd ever tried before. Silver, however, tipped his back in one go.

'Larry, that is **_INCREDIBLE_** ... the best thing I've ever tasted!'

'It certainly is – finest milk in the land, warms the belly. Which you'll need when you hear what I have to tell you.'

Larry sat on the corner of his desk nursing his drink, as the kittens took up their seats in the cosy leather chairs facing him.

'Toto,' he began, 'do you know why I've called you here today?'

'Larry, Larry,' Silver interrupted, eager to get on Larry's good side. 'Boss-man, head honcho, big guy, I think you'll find you called, **US**, as in Toto **AND ME** ... Silver! Am I right or am I right?'

He turned to his sister, who looked back at him, appalled.

Ignoring her, he continued, 'I'm sure you know Toto and I are a team. And just to reassure you, I'm **KIND** of a **NINJA** now too. I pretty much have all the skills and know what to do ... Shut your eyes, clear your mind, beat up the bad guys etc. etc..'

Toto put her head in her paws out of embarrassment.

'Err, right,' said Larry. 'I'm sure you're invaluable Silver, but let's all focus.'

'Gotcha, boss.' Silver gave Larry two thumbs up and a wink. He looked very pleased with himself as he eased himself back into the chair, and knocked back another glass of creamy milk.

Larry seemed a little puzzled, but continued. 'Toto, I couldn't let on when I first met you, but I knew that you were the newest member of the **ANCIENT ORDER OF INTERNATIONAL NINJA CATS**. I am head of the UK branch. In fact, I was trained by the very cat who trained you, your old master Ventura, back in Italy. Who, I might say, speaks very highly of you.'

'Yeah, he's a great,' said Silver. 'Taught

us everything we know ...' He trailed off as he caught sight of Toto's face. She was sporting a look that could kill, and had even unsheathed her claws!

'As I was saying, Toto,' Larry continued, 'after your excellent work capturing Brian the snake, the time has come to tell you exactly what the Order is, and where, as our newest member, you come in.'

'We're all ears,' said Silver, his legs over the armchair, as he sneakily helped himself to yet another glass of Jersey milk.

Toto ignored her brother and nodded seriously. This was it, the mission she had been trained for. She could feel her heart beating faster in her chest.

'The Ancient Order of International

Ninja Cats has been serving the world and preserving harmony for over two hundred years. Our founders saw that human kind simply couldn't be trusted to run the world without a little help. You see with humans it's all ego and pride, which leads to conflict.

'So, ninja cats were appointed for every major world leader. And each time a prime minister, a monarch or a president gets a little hot under the collar and is about to do something stupid … Well, we do what cats have always done. We act cute, sit on their laps, purr, bring their heart rate down, you know, all the stuff that relaxes humans, and stops them from doing anything rash. In short, without us, the world would be a mess.'

'It's **GENIUS**,' said Toto.

'It certainly is. To date we've stopped twenty world wars, thirty-two states of emergency and countless diplomatic incidents. There was a pretty close call with some mob bosses and the Americans last week – thank goodness for my American counterpart, Tex!'

'But where does the ninja training come in?' asked Toto.

'There are times when even a tummy tickle, a nuzzle and some purrs won't fix the situation. Then, we have to take secret action with our paws and if necessary, our claws. Of course, we all have cover stories, so to the wider world I am Chief Mouser, Head of Guest Liaison, Head of Feline

Security, and Head of Quality Control for All Antique Furniture of a Napping Standard.'

'It sounds like you have all the important jobs!' said Toto.

'Well, yes. And I am in dire need of a deputy, so when my old master Ventura told me about you, I knew I wanted you on my team. And now I have a rather urgent mission for you.' Larry turned to pour himself another glass of milk, only to find the decanter had been drained ...

Silver licked his whiskers guiltily and quickly blurted out, 'An **URGENT MISSION!** What's the plan? Is it close protection for the royal cat wedding perhaps? I read that a beautiful American Shorthair is engaged to our handsome

British Blue Prince. Lovely couple.'

'I'm afraid it's far more serious than that,' replied Larry looking grim. 'Kittens, in just a few days, we welcome an international peace conference to London. We are hosting it and, for humans and animals alike, it needs to go smoothly. I don't need to tell you that we live in dangerous times.'

'If the ninja cats are here, what can go wrong?' asked Toto.

'Alas, there are things that even we can't control,' he said, shaking his head. 'Brace yourselves, because I'm getting to the concerning news. At these conferences the British Prime Ministers have always laid on superb food and drink – it's one of the things we're famous for. Fresh salmon from

Scotland, the finest Hereford roast beef, sweet Kentish strawberries and cream ...'

'I'm there, I'm so there,' murmured Silver, rolling onto his back in the armchair in some kind of food trance.

'Sorry about him, please continue,' said Toto.

'It's all topped off with cheese,' said Larry. 'Mountains of it! The finest cheese board in the world. I can't tell you how many international crises have been saved by this cheese board, it's a thing of mystery and beauty.'

'Really?' asked Toto. 'Humans can't just solve their differences by talking and being reasonable?'

CHEESEY WHIFF!

'That is a good point, but they are rather slow on the uptake ... and, you know, the cheese helps,'

'I get it, sis,' piped up Silver, who looked

like he'd returned from his food trance and was back in the room. 'Who doesn't love cheese?'

'And that's the problem,' said Larry. 'There isn't any.'

'You've run out of cheese?' asked Silver. 'What a funny coincidence; we had exactly the same problem earlier today!'

'Not run out, it's much more serious than that. I'm saying that every single piece of cheese in the UK has been stolen on the eve of the most important peace conference in years, and with it might go the best shot we've got at keeping the human leaders, and therefore the world, peaceful and happy ... In short, we are in trouble, and I need you to help.'

'That explains our fridge!' said Toto, 'So that's our mission? To find the cheese?'

'Exactly. I only have one lead, but I can't follow it up because my face is too well-known. We have a tip-off that a cut-throat smuggler cat has information and is prepared to make a trade. You'll need to meet him at the Sour Saucer – a notorious milk bar by the river.'

'That doesn't sound too hard, right sis?' said Silver, sounding a tad cocky. 'We go to the bar, turn the charm on, get the cheese back to Number 10, save the day, become heroes … **BOOM** … Don't leave me hanging,' he said to Toto holding out his paw.

But Toto **DID** leave him hanging – she could see from Larry's face that he wasn't finished, and the news didn't look good.

'I'm afraid I need you to go undercover and promise not to use any ninja fighting skills. If this smuggler finds out you're a ninja it'll spook him and we'll never get the cheese back.'

'Larry, will you relax,' said Silver. 'We've got this! Charm is my middle name, we'll have the formaggio back by tea time, so polish up the medals and tell the royal couple to stick us down on the invite list, because we are saving the day ...'

While Silver was excited, confident and couldn't wait to get going, Toto felt unusually scared and nervous. This was her first **PROPER MISSION** and she didn't want to let her new boss down. But what was she supposed to do if she couldn't use the very skills she'd acquired to do the job in the first place?

Larry continued. 'The cat you are going to meet is called Elias Copinger. He's big, mean and grey with a streak of black fur from his nose to his tail. When you make contact, he'll ask you your favourite drink, you need to answer with the code word: **"CONDENSED MILK"**. This will be the key for him to give you the information. Do whatever you can to get the intel, and get out of there. There's no time to waste: we need that cheese back.'

ELIAS COPINGER

Silver and Toto rose from their chairs, stood to attention and saluted. Larry returned the salute, and stared down at the two kittens.

'The international ninja cat motto has always been **"PURRS, PAWS AND CLAWS"**, because that's what we use to preserve peace and harmony, and always in that order. If purrs don't work, we use paws and if paws don't work ... well you get the picture ...'

'PURRS, PAWS AND CLAWS!' the cats repeated in unison.

'That's the spirit. Good luck.' Larry smiled. 'And Silver ...'

'Yes?'

' ... maybe lose the hat.'

CHAPTER 5

The cats left Number 10 as the summer sun was beginning to fade. They followed their noses through a warren of alleyways down to the river, towards the Sour Saucer.

The riverside milk bar (a bit like a human pub) was directly underneath Blackfriars bridge on the north side of the Thames. It was right near the waterline, and almost completely hidden from human eyes. It

had been there since Victorian times and was the legendary stop off where scores of thirsty animals used to have their final drink before boarding ships bound for lives in the new worlds of America or Australia. All animals were welcome: cats, rats, dogs, you name it. They all drank (and fought) here.

It took its name from the beverage that had made the milk bar famous. It was said that if you could drink the sour saucer of milk in one go without turning green, you were worthy of a place on board a ship. If not, you had to walk the plank from the bar, straight out, **SPLASH**, into the Thames.

Toto and Silver could hear fog horns and the sound of seagulls squawking as they descended the steps to the entrance of the milk bar. The sun had set now and there was a chilly summer fog where the warm air met the cold river. They could just about see the lights from the top of the Shard in one direction and the Houses of Parliament in the other.

'Ok, sis, I'll do the talking,' said Silver. 'It's the one thing I know I can do.'

'That's probably for the best,' replied Toto. 'I'll only be able to see this Elias Copinger up close, and me going from cat to cat staring might draw attention to us.'

'Quite right. You stay by the door and let me scope the place. I'll call you over when I've found the guy.'

'Just one thing though, Silver, you can

talk for Italy ... Please **DON'T** talk your way into trouble. Just use the code word for the all important information and then we can get out of here.'

'Trust me,' Silver said with a wink as he opened the door, and together the cats slipped into the dim room beyond.

The packed bar had a low ceiling with wooden beams and it was lit completely by candle light. There were several long tables in the centre of the room and countless booths in the nooks and crannies along the walls where the patrons ate and drank and whispered in the shadows to each other. A band made up of two cats on violins, a Saint Bernard dog on double bass, and a skinny rat on accordion played in the left corner.

CATS ← WC → DOGS

I ♥ LONDON

To the right there was a dark wooden bar with a mirror behind it that stretched the length of the pub. There were several types of milk served on tap and countless other barrels and bottles of the creamy stuff lined up behind the gruff-looking bartender – an enormous tabby Maine Coon, who looked like he shouldn't be messed with.

Silver sidled up to the bar and, trying to act as confidently as he could, ordered two glasses of house milk.

'Bit young to be in here, aren't you?' the bartender asked as he placed the glasses on the bar with a thud, sloshing milk over the edge.

'**MAMMA MIA!** I thought Britannia was supposed to rule the sea? Me and my sister are from Italy – we start our sailors young,' Silver said in a ridiculously exaggerated Italian accent.

The bartender grunted, which seemed to give Silver encouragement to embelish his story.

'Yes, we've been over here a while; came on a shipment of smuggled pistachios. Since then we've done some work as hired muscle for the Rattinoffs up in Camden, but we're looking to get back on the sea.'

Silver turned and gave Toto a thumbs up. By the door, his sister groaned inwardly and hoped for the best.

'We heard about this place, and that there might be work going. We were told to ask for an Elias Copinger, do you know where we can find him?'

'Are you sure you want to sail with him?' asked the bartender, raising his bushy eyebrows. 'He's one of the toughest smugglers there is. There's more than one cat who's crossed him and ended up at the bottom of the Thames.'

'Hey, whatta can I say? We wantta to sail with the bestta!' said Silver, taking his Italian accent to the extreme. He knocked back his milk and put on a brave face.

'All right, it's your funeral. He's that mean-looking cat over there in the corner. Good luck ... strange lad,' he muttered as he sloped off to serve another customer.

'We're in,' said Silver to Toto, as he made his way back to the door. 'But my word he looks tough.'

Just as Larry had described, Elias was dark grey with a streak of jet black, and he was also missing half an ear – it looked like it had been torn from his head. What marked him out at the moment, though, was the poor cat he held by the throat, paws dangling in mid-air, who only a minute ago he had been playing cards with.

'You little creep, I saw you switch cards.

No one cheats at this table apart from me.'

The table of rough-looking cats, rats and a ferret burst out laughing. The poor misfortunate cat frantically looked around for someone to help him. Toto could barely resist stepping in. She moved to intervene, but Silver stopped her.

'Are you mad, sis? You can't blow your cover! Besides, that cat's made his own bed, this isn't your fight.'

Toto desperately wanted to give this bully a taste of his own medicine, but she knew her brother was speaking sense. She had to focus on her mission.

'GET OUT OF MY SIGHT!' screamed Elias and threw the poor cat straight out of the window, into the gloomy river below.

'Can he swim?' asked one of his goons.

'What do I care?' said Elias with a cackle, and returned to his card game.

'Well ... that was a nice introduction ... what a charming man,' said Silver nervously. 'Wish me luck, sis.'

'Be careful—' whispered Toto, but it was too late – Silver was already striding through the crowd towards their target.

'Mr Copinger?' Silver asked as he approached the table where the gang of sailors and smugglers were seated.

'Who wants to know?' asked Elias over his shoulder.

'Err. My name is ...' Silver stuttered, desperately trying to think of a fake name, 'Christopher, and over there,' he said, pointing to Toto, 'is my sister, err ... Columbus.'

The big cat turned and looked the kittens up and down, which was not too hard as he was about ten times the size of the furry duo.

'You what? Your parents called you **CHRISTOPHER AND COLUMBUS?** Were they having a laugh? Nice to meet you mate, I'm Sir Francis Drake.'

His gang burst out laughing again. Silver joined in with a forced chuckle, hoping he was blending in.

'My sister and I want to work for you and we were hoping to have a **DRINK** and discuss the prospect,' he said, knowingly touching his nose and hoping this would give him a chance to slip the code word in.

'Well, before I could even think of interviewing you for a job, you both have to pass the basic test of the *SOUR SAUCER*. Henry! Two of your finest please, and get – Columbus, is it? – over here now.' Toto joined her brother as the landlord brought over the foulest concoction the cats had ever smelled. It was milk, yes, but it was so off you could almost stand in it. The bartender smiled apologetically.

'Excellent. Down the hatch you two,' said Elias, 'then we'll start to think about you sailing with us. If not ... *THEN IT'S THE PLANK* for you.' He pointed menacingly towards the window that the last poor cat had been thrown out of. The bar suddenly

hushed as all eyes turned to the kittens.

'Cheers, sis,' laughed Silver nervously as they clinked glasses.

Toto paused and tried not to gag at the smell wafting up from the curdled milk. Being blind meant Toto's sense of smell was far stronger than her brother's.

It was like nothing Toto had ever tasted, or wanted to ever again. It was smelly, thick, a bit chewy – you couldn't really call it a drink. In short, it was **_DISGUSTING_**. Toto knew she had to keep it down or they'd never find out where the cheese was, but it was one of the hardest things she'd ever had to do. She looked over to Silver but incredibly it seemed he was actually **_ENJOYING IT!_**

'That hit the spot,' said Silver and it was clear he meant it. 'Fire in the belly, arrrgh!'

'Blimey! All right you two,' said Elias, obviously impressed. 'Pull up a chair and let me get you a real drink. What will you have?'

'Thank you, Mr Copinger, our favourite drink is ... **_CONDENSED MILK_**,' said Toto.

'What was that?' the big cat asked, suddenly looking suspicious.

'She said our **FAVOURITE DRINK** is **CONDENSED MILK**,' Silver said loudly, like he was really pleased with himself.

Elias rose from the table, as did all his gang, and indeed half the pub. Everyone was focused on the two small cats ...

'Ah, the guests we've been waiting for. Although, not in the way you were hoping. You made a mistake coming in here my little stowaways. My boss told me to expect someone trying to find out all sorts about our business ... Boys, time to see if these two can swim.'

Before Silver could squeak 'it's a trap!', he was picked up by one of Elias's goons and thrown across the room, crashing across tables and landing on the floor on the other side of the bar.

This is going to hurt, thought Toto as, with one massive paw, Elias sent her flying across the room after her brother.

'Ouch! That guy hits like a truck,' she said, shaking her head, as she and Silver hid behind the overturned table.

'I'm not sure how we get out of this,' whispered Silver.

'Tell me about it!' hissed Toto. 'This guy has double-crossed us, which means we're not getting any clues about where the cheese is. Plus I'm not supposed to use any of my ninja skills ... even though I *REALLY* want to, as this guy is asking for a wallop!' she said, looking angry. 'Silver, I think we'll have to fight, or we'll end up in the Thames. But I can't disobey a direct order from Larry, so we'll have to scrap like ordinary alley cats and then make a break for the door. Ready?'

'Ready,' replied Silver.

She had to hand it to her brother, he might not be a ninja, but he was as brave as one.

'On my count, over the table in **3 ... 2, ... 1 ... NOW!**'

The cats pushed over the table, ready to fight with paws up and claws out.

'Oh ... that wasn't what I was hoping for,' said Silver.

Instead of the small gang from Elias's table, the kittens now had the whole bar facing them. Forty cut-throats, all looking very dangerous.

'We're dead,' whispered Silver.

Toto agreed. Even if she used her ninja skills these were going to be tough opponents. And what would Larry say when he found out she'd had to break her cover?

'Say your prayers, Christopher and Columbus,' said Elias. 'You are off to Davy Jones's locker!'

The kittens looked at each other blankly.

'Oh, for kitty's sake! It's an old sailors' term – it means you're going to a watery grave ... never mind, get them!'

'**EXCUSE ME**, you appear not to be extending our our famous London hospitality to our new friends.' All heads turned to a solitary figure standing on top of the bar. Dressed in a dark blue trench coat and wearing a wide brimmed fedora hat which obscured his face, no one could quite see who the intruder to the party was.

'**ARRRGH ... WHO ARE YOU?**' asked the frustrated Elias. 'Can't I be left in peace for one second whilst I drown these traitors!'

'I'm afraid I can't let you do that dear boy, simply wouldn't be sporting.'

'Fine,' sighed Elias, 'one more cat going for a swim. **_GET HI_**—' Before he could finish the sentence, the intruder jumped off the bar, swung on a medieval-looking chandelier and launched himself at Elias. His boot connected with the big cat's face and sent him tumbling out of the window. Elias screamed in fury as he splashed into the cold water below. The intruder landed deftly in front of the kittens.

The band of cut-throats stared gobsmacked, unsure what to do without their bullying leader.

Then a wiry ferret screamed **_'CHARGE!'_**

and they all rushed towards the mystery hero.

He disappeared in a scrum of paws and claws as the cut-throats tried to take him down. Silver winced, but Toto leaped towards the scrap. 'Sorry Larry, but it looks like I'll have to blow my cover, I've got to help!' she said to herself.

What followed was a brief but brilliant thirty-second display of ninja awesomeness. All the other animals seemed to be moving in slow motion as Toto easily ducked and swerved. Every punch and kick that was thrown missed her. She sent a couple of rats flying, before dodging out of the way of two dogs leaving them to crash into each other. A ferret twisted herself into a knot trying to catch Toto's tail as she scissor-kicked a gruff-looking squirrel. Finally, Toto picked up a hedgehog and took out the last

three gang members like they were pins in a bowling alley.

'Come on!' Toto yelped, pulling the mystery hero to his feet. 'Let's get out of here!'

Silver ran to join them and they raced

to the door, leaving the gang sprawling on the floor in the carnage of smashed milk bottles.

'We need to warn the boss that there was a ninja here!' a voice called out behind them. **'THE ORDER IS ONTO US!'**

CHAPTER 6

Toto, Silver and the helpful stranger ran breathlessly along the riverbank, and then ducked into a shadowy alleyway.

'Well, that was impressive and very brave,' Toto said gratefully.

'Yes,' added Silver. 'But how did you know we were in trouble? And why did you help us? And **WHO ARE YOU?**'

'Well, this is one of my local bars, and I've

always hated that bully Elias. So, when I saw there was a spot of bother, I thought I'd come and lend a hand. Even though I know you know how to look after yourself, Toto.'

'How do you who I am?' gasped the small, furry ninja.

'Oh, that's quite simple my dear ... I'm one of your closest friends,' he said, taking off the hat and bowing in a grand sweeping gesture.

TA-DAH

'CATFACE!' the kittens said in unison, and jumped on him, nuzzling his face.

They were over the moon to see their friend, but Toto still felt confused: 'But you hate fighting? And why are you in disguise?'

'After my frankly weedy attempt at fighting in our last adventure, I've been getting self-defence lessons from Brenda, the King Cobra. And the disguise? Well, I happened to run into Larry earlier, and I thought I'd do my own investigating into this missing cheese. It affects us all you know – very serious business.'

'I'd forgotten about the cheese,' said Silver, piteously. 'We have no clue where it is. And since our informant double-crossed us, the bad guys will know all about us but we know nothing about them! It's hopeless.'

'That might not be entirely true, brother. When Elias was about to give me a good right hook, I pilfered this from his pocket,' said Toto, producing a crumpled piece of paper from her closed up paw.

'You're a **GENIUS** sis, I bet it's a clue!'

Catface, got his reading glasses out of his jacket pocket. 'Ah! It's a peckergram, It's what humans call telegrams – but here in London, the woodpeckers of the royal parks create the telegrams with their beaks. Now, let me see, "Shipment of Fromage STOP Leaving Greenwich STOP Midnight STOP Bring crackers and grapes for journey STOP And something warm to wear STOP Wouldn't want you to catch cold STOP

Lots of love **ADF** STOP".'

The colour drained from his face as he read the last three letters.

'What is it Catface? This is great news, the cheese must be in Greenwich ... wherever that is,' said Toto.

'Yes, but I'm also pretty certain I know who's behind it, and it's not good news. There's not a moment to spare,' he said as he looked at his watch. '11pm. We need to get moving and fast! But you're going to need new disguises, or they'll recognise us. Luckily, after my chat with Larry I came prepared.'

From beneath his coat Catface brought out a couple of stripy Breton tops as well as bandanas. He tied these around the kittens' heads and stepped back to admire his handiwork.

'Oh, that is quite something, even old Elias himself would think you were part of his motley band! Now for our transport ...'

Catface launched himself at a nearby lamppost. He climbed to the top, where he perched and started making the strangest and most ungodly **SQUAWK** the kittens had ever heard in their lives. Toto and Silver held their paws to their ears in shock. What on earth was he doing?

Then, through the misty night air, three shapes began to materialise. They were vague at first but they began to get **CLOSER** and **BIGGER** and **SCARIER!**

'Catface,' a shrieking voice said out of the

darkness, 'this better be good! We were fast asleep, getting ready for an early start at Billingsgate Fish Market.'

'MARY!' The kittens rushed forward as the big seagull landed in front of them. She gave them a cuddle with her enormous wings.

Mary was queen of the gulls in London, and had met the kittens on their first adventure when Catface had shown them around the city.

'It's good to see you two little ones again. Though, gosh, you've grown! I do hope you'll still fit on.' Mary stepped back and added, 'now, allow me to introduce my babies: Laura and Mews.'

Two younger gulls appeared from behind her. '**DUDES!!!** You kitties ready to grab some air?' one said, then high fived the cats with his wing tip.

'Catface,' said Mary, 'you said you needed three gulls, and here we are. Although your seagull is so bad you could have asking for three guinea pigs! Why don't you just speak normally?'

'Oh dear, is it really that bad? I'm mortified. It's just that we need to get to Greenwich on an urgent mission for Larry, and I couldn't think how else to get hold of you!'

'All right, all right, hop on. And you two,' she pointed a wing at the younger gulls, 'if you even think of trying any of that adrenalin junkie stuff with these poor kittens on your backs, you'll be on cod heads all week, do I make myself clear?'

'DUDE, CHILLAX,' squawked Mews. **'STOP CALLING ME DUDE ... I'M YOUR MOTHER.'**

'OK ... *dudette*,' the young gull murmured out of earshot, smirking to his sister before they launched into the misty night.

The gulls glided expertly in formation through the summer fog, and levelled off just before they hit the river. They swooped so low that the cats' paws could have touched

the water (not that they'd ever do such a thing.
Cats and water? Not the best of friends).

Laura turned to see if Toto was nervous,
but it was clear the little cat was loving
every second. Toto knew she needed to stay
calm and focus on the mission ahead of her,
but with the wind rushing through her big
mane she couldn't help but feel excited.

They passed barges and late-night revellers on pleasure boats. And as they flew on, the mist gradually cleared to give them a great view of the the city lights. To the left were lots of skyscrapers, to the right the old warship HMS Belfast and, dead ahead, the king of all London bridges: Tower Bridge.

'Mum, I know we're in a bit of a hurry, but permission to show these cats some tricks?' asked Laura.

'Seeing as you didn't call me "dude", permission granted. But get back here in formation ASAP, we've got a job to do.'

'You two little dudes are going to love this,' Mews shouted.

The gulls flew under the bridge, immediately shot up vertically to the top of the towers where they hovered for a moment in the air, before free falling down to the river below. It was a perfect **_LOOP THE LOOP!_** They finished by gliding expertly back into formation alongside their mother.

'**_MEOWAAAAAARRRGGHHHH,_**' Toto and

Silver screamed.

'**WHAT A RUSH!** You dudes enjoy?' they asked the kittens.

Silver looked green, but he had to admit it was exciting.

Toto was beaming from ear to ear. 'This is the **BEST** way to travel, right Catface?'

'I should say,' laughed Catface. 'But these gulls don't ferry just *anyone* around. They're far too independent. We are hugely privileged.'

Then he called out to Mary, 'I need to talk to these young'uns, let's close ranks.'

'Roger that.' She said. The gulls flew impressively close to each other. Over the whooshing of the gulls' wings, Catface began his brief.

'Toto, Silver, this will be like nothing you've faced before. The King Cobras were a cake walk, or should I say, a "snakewalk", compared to this ... I say, that's rather good isn't it?' he said smiling.

The kittens stared at him, just a little confused.

'Sorry. *Focus, Catface.* **A**, **D** and **F**, are the initials used by one of the greatest ninjas ever to be a member of your Order, Toto. He is lightning fast, and so silent he once snuck up on an elite army of Siamese cats without them hearing even the sound of his breath. He is very intelligent, too – he won the final of that TV show *Catsamind* ... twice!'

'If he's a ninja, there must be some mistake. We're the **GOOD GUYS.** Surely this is all a misunderstanding?' asked Toto, almost pleading for this to be true.

'Alas, no,' Catface replied. 'There's no mistake. He was banished and we thought we'd never see him again, but this proves he's back.'

'Catface,' piped up Silver, 'what does **ADF** stand for?'

'It's an abbreviation of his name: **ARCHDUKE FERDICAT.**'

'What is it with this country and your weird names?' asked Silver.

'He's cat royalty, that's where the **ARCHDUKE** comes in, and **FERDICAT** is a family name. It's quite fabulous really. What's more, he's terribly handsome. He always wears a dashing black cape and, as

is his family tradition, carries a rapier sword. He's the finest swordsman in the whole of Europe, never been bested.'

'So, what happened?' asked Toto, eager to find out why this great ninja had fallen from grace.

'After they finished their training and Larry got the job at Number 10, he and Ferdicat just didn't see eye to eye on the role of the ninja cats. Ferdy ... well let's just say he's not as keen on humans as the rest of your order. He thinks cats would do a better job of running things. I mean, he's probably right, but we're all on the same planet, and humans have their uses, so it's good to live and let live.

'Anyway, things came to a head, and it's said that Larry inflicted the only defeat in combat Ferdy has ever suffered. He's been living his life in exile ever since, so what he has to do with all this missing cheese is anyone's guess.'

Catface looked up and spotted the famous Greenwich landmark up ahead – a very old ship called the Cutty Sark.

'Mary, make for the old warehouses. We have to get in undetected.'

'Leave that to us my friend,' said Mary, as the three seagulls expertly circled the docks.

'This place is teeming with guards,' Mews observed.

The gulls glided silently over the sloped rooftops of the warehouses, searching for somewhere they could land unseen. But scores of cats were patrolling, dressed much like the ones in the bar and armed with menacing-looking rolling pins.

'Toto, you might need to show us some of those skills I hear you're famous for ...' whispered Laura.

'Of course!' replied Toto.

The young gull started to spiral slowly downwards until she was directly above two big and scary looking cats guarding a rooftop below.

'Get ready to jump. *3*, *2*, *1* ... *GO!*'

The ninja cat leaped headfirst towards the shadows she could just about make out

WHOOOSH

beneath her. As she approached the first guard she swung her body so she was upright then deftly bounced off of his shoulders, using him like a trampoline to jump into the night air again. He looked around, bewildered about what had just landed on him. He didn't have to wait too long to find out. Toto descended again with a

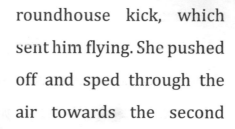

roundhouse kick, which sent him flying. She pushed off and sped through the air towards the second

SWOOSH

BOP

OOF

guard. He turned just in time to see a blur of Toto's Breton top before her paw knocked him into next week. The ninja then landed silently and effortlessly on her back paws.

'That felt good!' she said, as her comrades landed next to her.

'That was truly **AWESOME** dude,' said Laura.

Toto smiled at her, then quickly took charge of the situation. 'Right, gulls, we need you to fly to Downing Street immediately. Tell Larry that **ARCHDUKE FERDICAT** is back and we're going to need reinforcements. We'll try and find out where the cheese is and make sure that ship doesn't set sail. OK?'

'Good plan, little cat', said Mary. 'But be

careful – if this **ARCHFERDIWHATSIT** is half as dangerous as Catface makes out, you best have your wits about you.'

The three gulls headed off into the night sky leaving Toto, Silver and Catface to face the deadliest of foes: one of Toto's own, a fellow **NINJA** warrior.

CHAPTER 7

Slowly and methodically,
the cats lowered themselves
down from the rooftop.
Catface almost slipped a
couple of times, so Toto
helped him out, but it
was clear his balance had
improved a lot during his
training with Brenda.

When they hit the ground, they hid in the shadows to get their bearings.

'OK Catface, where now?' Toto asked.

'My instinct says this way,' he said, pointing to the right where row after row of old warehouses jutted out into the river. 'My father used to bring me here all the time when he was smuggling cheese himself back in the day. If we get challenged remember to act, well, you know, *CUT-THROATY*.'

Unfortunately, as they slunk around the corner trying to look as cut-throaty as possible, they came face-to-face with an enormous, growling, salivating, ferocious, and worryingly *HUNGRY-LOOKING* Doberman dog.

GRRRRRRRR

'No one move a muscle,' whispered Silver, although there was no danger of that for Catface. He looked like he'd been frozen into a rat statue!

'I don't recognise you rapscallions,' the beast growled, her eyes narrowing. She looked like she wanted to devour them. 'Tell me, What's the best way to enjoy **NORWEGIAN PRAWNS?**'

'Err,' Silver spluttered. He turned to see if his sister had an answer to this strange question, but there was no one in the place she'd been standing half a second ago.

Instead, there was a whirl of black and brown fur whizzing past his ear, as Toto launched herself right at the dog's fearsome jaws.

'Wait, Toto, **DON'T!**' Catface shouted, aghast. But it was too late, the little ninja's back foot connected with the big dog and shot her back through a crate of wooden pallets knocking her clean out.

'Have you lost your mind, Catface?' asked Silver. 'That thing was going to kill us.'

'Actually, I rather think *she* wasn't,' Catface replied as the group gathered around the passed-out dog. 'That was the code question for our undercover police force. Oh, if only I'd realised sooner ... she's on our side!'

Catface shook the dog gently to try and revive her. 'Mayo – the best way to enjoy Norwegian prawns is with mayo!' he muttered.

'Oh no, we're not working with *A DOG!*' moaned Silver. 'Listen – I might be greedy. And you, Catface, are quite vain.'

'Well you do have me there,' admitted Catface.

'But,' continued Silver, 'dogs are idiots, they simply can't be trusted. They're too **EXCITABLE**, they **LICK EVERYONE**, and frankly, they **SMELL**. We cannot buddy up with a dog on Toto's first mission.'

'Well it might be **YOUR** first mission, but let me assure you it's **NOT** mine,' the Doberman retorted, catching them all by surprise as she sat up and rubbed her head. 'So, if you'd be so kind, please don't do that again, it really hurt.'

'Sorry about that, the training kicked in,' said Toto.

'No hard feelings. I'm sorry about the whole "grr, angry dog thing" – you gave me a start when you came around the corner. I'm undercover, so got to stay in character and

///

all that jazz. Oh, where are my manners? I'm Shelia Snarlingfoot, **CIA**.'

'**CIA?**' asked Silver.

'**C**riminal **I**nvestigation **A**nimals. The humans just think we're police dogs, but we run our own cases on the side. We're an interspecies department so we work with cats all the time, in fact my boss is a cat.'

'No surprise there,' muttered Silver to Toto under his breath.

The cats went to shake paws, but Shelia had other ideas, and gave all three a big lick.

'See, Catface: licks! Argh, gross,' cried Silver.

'Sorry, force of habit ... It's a dog thing.'

'No sweat, so what have you heard about **ADF?**' asked Toto.

'Well, I haven't been able to get too close, he only seems to share his plans with a few trusted henchmen, especially this mean grey cat with one ear.'

'Elias,' said Toto.

'Yes, that's the one. Turned up here half an hour ago soaking wet and in a terrible mood. There have been other hired goons turning up all day with big containers but I haven't been able to get close enough to find out what's in them.'

'**THE CHEESE!**' said Silver. 'It must be.'

Toto quickly filled Sheila in on the potential catastrophe at Downing Street.

'Goodness,' said the Doberman. 'I had no idea it was that big, we just heard *ADF* was back and wanted to see what he was up to. This explains why he's got such a big ship! It seems that the Archduke has been recruiting an army; there's a good hundred cats and rats on board. But what can he be planning to do?'

'I don't know,' said Toto, 'but we need to get onto that boat, find the cheese and make sure it doesn't leave port, otherwise we could have a **MAJOR INTERNATIONAL CRISIS** on our hands.'

'That won't be easy. They've got Rottweilers guarding the gangway. They're tough, mean and on full alert. Plus, you'll stand out as they know most of the crew by sight ... But leave it with me – you just pick up some crates of supplies from the quartermaster and go to walk on board like it's your job. Sound like a plan?'

'That it does,' answered Toto. 'OK, you two, ready?'

'I'm not entirely sure I am. Even with my self-defence classes, this is more than I bargained for.' Catface looked nervous.

'We're with you sis,' said Silver. 'Come on, Catface, if we pull this off, you'll be the most popular cat-rat in London!'

'But I'm already the most— Oh, what the heck, let's go.'

'Good luck,' said Shelia, and gave them all a big lick of her pink tongue.

'*SHELIA!*' complained Silver.

'Sorry,' the big dog apologised. 'But, you know, take it as a compliment!'

And with that, the motley crew of cats,

rat and dog headed for the ship that was moored in the distance, not knowing what dangers they might face.

CHAPTER 8

'Come on ye 'orrible lot, get those supplies on board, The Flyin' Fish sets sail at midnight – quit yer yabberin' and get a move on!'

That was the cry from the quartermaster, an old Siberian cat in a tatty white sailor's jumper and a captain's cap. He was busy checking all the supplies at the end of the quay with a clipboard.

Approaching from the shadows, Toto

and the gang saw the ship for the first time. It was an enormous grey cargo ship, with twinkling lights showing through the portholes. Behind it lay the fast-flowing river where the tide was starting to take hold. Further out, it looked like the water was flowing around several small dark islands.

Several rough-looking cats were picking up boxes of supplies and carrying them up the gangway onto the ship. There was so much going on and so many animals coming and going that, with their disguises, they were able to get into line unnoticed and pick up three boxes full of canned tuna.

"old it you lot, I 'aven't seen ye before, what 'ave ye got there?' the quartermaster piped up in his impressively sea-faring voice as the trio turned to walk towards the ship.

'**ARRRGH** ... we been reassigned from rooftop security, and we be carryin' tuna bound for that there ship. We be needin' to know where to be puttin' it sir,' answered Catface in the worst pirate's accent the cats had ever heard – or so they thought!

'**ARRRGH** ... one of me own,' replied the quartermaster. 'It's good to be servin' with an old ship's cat such as yerself. Tell me, where did ye serve in the olden days?'

'Oh, no, we're for it now,' whispered Toto to Silver.

'Ah, well I started life as ship's cat on the HMS ... err, Sea Bass, and then served me time on the Platypus, before being shipwrecked in Tahiti. I been sailin' with the Archduke for a couple of months now, and can't wait to get me bounty in cheese! **ARRRGH** ...' he added for good measure.

The quartermaster eyed the trio for what seemed like an eternity. Both Toto and Silver had started to think the game was up when he replied with a yell, '**ARRRGH**, that's me kind of sailor, on ye go boys. Take that tuna down to the hold and good luck to ye.'

Counting their blessings, they scurried towards the ship.

'Catface, how in the world did you know all of those ships? And how did he fall for that awful accent?' asked Toto.

'What do you mean, **AWFUL?** That's what all the old pirates sound like in the Sour Saucer. As for the ships – I told you I used be down here all the time with my dad. I loved watching the ships come in when—'

'Guys, we've got a whole new problem,' Silver interrupted, pointing to the ship with a shaky paw.

Sure enough, guarding the gangway were two enormous Rottweilers.

'How in the world is Sheila going to deal with them?'

Just then, Shelia emerged from behind a big wooden container and appeared to be having a cheerful chat with them. It looked like she was asking the two bigger dogs to follow her. Miraculously they did, leaving

GRRRRRRR

the coast clear.

'Quick, get up the gangway,' urged Catface.

But as the cats boarded the ship, Toto heard distant growls and sensed that their new friend had bitten off more than she could chew. **'SHE'S IN TROUBLE!'**

'Sis, you've got to help her out,' pleaded Silver. 'She might be a dog, but she's **OUR** dog.'

'I'm way ahead of you, bro!'

Toto sprang onto the handrail of the ship, then took an almighty jump onto the nearby shipping containers.

Between two of the containers, she could fuzzily make out the shapes of the dogs below her.

The Rottweilers had Shelia pinned against the floor. They'd clearly seen through her cover story, and they looked deadly.

Toto knew that she'd only get one shot at this. If she mistimed her jump and failed to strike a decent blow, she'd get savaged by their fearsome fangs.

Her training kicked in: she cleared her mind, took a deep breath, launched to the

ground in a spin and
... ***DIRECT HIT!*** She
sent one dog hurling
through the air with
her flying kick, straight
into the river.

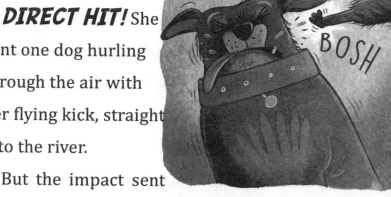

But the impact sent
Toto rolling across the floor, and the other
Rottweiler reacted quickly to catch her
off-guard before she could get to her feet.
It was as much as she could do to keep his
SLOBBERING jaws away from her head.
She knew he was far stronger that she was.
How was she going to get out of this one?

'We expected some trouble tonight,' the
dog snarled, 'but I didn't think the scrap
would be this easy. The boss will be over

the moon when I bring your fluffy hide to him.'

Toto knew she didn't have much time before dog's jaws closed in around her. Pinned beneath the massive beast, her strength was waning, but she took aim and brought her hind paw up in a sharp jab.

'OOOWWWWWW!'

he yelled in agony, and loosened his grip just enough for Toto to push him off with her legs. He, too, was sent sprawling off the quay into the water.

'That was close! Are you OK?' Toto

asked Shelia.

'Just about, boy they were strong. How can I repay you? You saved my bacon!'

'Well, so long as you don't lick me, let's call it quits,' said Toto with a wink. 'Right, you go and scout for Larry – bring him on board when he gets here if you can? And we'll try and find this cheese.'

Sheila saluted, then trotted back towards the docks leaving Toto to board the ship again.

Silver passed her a box of tuna saying, 'wow, not strictly a ninja move, but good street fighting sis.'

Catface gave her a welcome pat on the back.

'Let's get going kittens, I'm sure the

cheese must be in the hold at the bottom of the boat.'

They made their way down the levels of the ship. With their disguises and the tuna in their arms no one seemed suspicious of them. Floor after floor they descended, until they reached a big iron door, right in the bowels of the boat.

Catface twisted the handle and they all pushed. The noise as they entered was deafening. The engines were clearly warming up in preparation for the journey ahead.

'I can't wait for this, I've missed cheese so much today! Do you think it would be OK if I had a bit – just a nibble?' asked Silver longingly.

'I don't think you'll even get that,' said Catface, quickly scanning the hold. **'THERE'S NO CHEESE HERE!'**

'What?' cried Toto. 'Where else could it be?'

'There are just cans and cans of tuna – hundreds of them to feed the crew. But not a morsel of cheese.'

'There must be another room down here where they're keeping it. Let's follow our noses!' Toto sent the team in different directions, and she closed her eyes to allow her sense of smell to take over ...

Silver tried hard to focus and search, but he soon found himself distracted by the scene out of a porthole. The night sky looked so beautiful reflected in the water moving by. He opened the round window to have a better look out and noticed countless huge dark shapes being pulled along by the ship.

'Hang on,' he said out loud to himself. 'Those islands are moving ... They aren't islands, they must be barges ... And they smell great. Wait a second: the cheese is on the barges! ***I'M A GENIUS!***'

He felt very pleased with himself for all of two seconds, until he realised something else. 'Oh no, I'm not a genius – we're leaving the docks!'

He ran to find Toto and Catface.

'I have excellent and very bad news, take your pick,' he said quickly.

'Well, I'll go excellent if I may,' answered Catface.

'I think I might have found the cheese.'

'You superstar!' said Toto. 'What could possibly be bad news after that?'

'I think we're already sailing ***OUT TO SEA!***'

CHAPTER 9

Toto snapped into action. Just because they were on a ship teeming with baddies, heading to goodness knows where, didn't necessarily mean she'd failed her first mission. She just had to figure out how to fix things.

'We need to quietly take command of this ship,' she told her friends. 'Catface, you know the most about ships – where do you steer from?'

Catface thought carefully for a moment. 'I expect the wheelhouse will be on the upper deck. There should be a ladder up to a hatch somewhere around here, they use it to lower goods straight down into the hold.'

They quickly found it and started the long climb upwards.

Finally, they reached the big hatch and cautiously pushed it open to peer out.

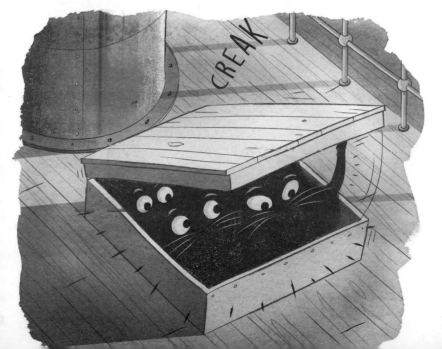

'Right ... not exactly the best news,' Catface whispered to Toto.

'Yeah, I can see figures – lots of figures,' said the ninja. 'Are they what I think they are?'

'I'm afraid so,' answered her ratty friend.

The whole of the ship's company was gathered on the deck. There were hundreds of cats, rats and dogs of all shapes and sizes. They were wearing similar outfits: stripy tops or old navy coats with caps or bandanas. They looked tough, mean, and like they knew how to fight.

Luckily, nobody noticed as the trio pulled themselves up onto the deck. All eyes were trained on the bridge of the boat, where their fearsome leader stood at the railings preparing to address his crew.

He was flanked by several other big cats including Elias and a pair of shifty-looking Siamese cats, but it was clear who was in charge.

He wore an enormous velvet top hat and a spectacular black cape that flapped in the sea breeze. At his waist, a black scabbard hung from a sword belt and the steel hilt of his rapier was just visible glistening in the moonlight. His face was black with a white nose and whiskers. It had to be ...

ARCHDUKE FERDICAT!

'Wow, he looks incredible,' Silver whispered, as he explained the scene to Toto. 'I would not want to fight this guy, he looks like he means business.'

'Hmm I love that outfit,' added Catface. 'I must find out where he got that cape.'

'*NOT HELPING*,' hissed Toto at the other two. 'Look, here's the plan: when he starts talking we use that as a distraction. Stick to the side of the ship and make for the wheelhouse. Then we turn this thing back to the docks. Where hopefully Larry should be waiting with back-up ... Let's go.'

The ship was now at the mouth of the Thames and heading out to sea. The wind was beginning to pick up and a storm was building on the dark horizon. Spray was starting to cover the deck as the ship steamed into the waves.

The kittens and Catface slowly shuffled round the edge of the crowd as the commanding cat started to address his crew.

'My dear cut-throats, smugglers, pirates and robbers, thank you for your hard work so far. Very soon, when I take over the world, you will all have riches beyond your wildest dreams.'

'HURRAH! HURRAH!' the meow went up from the crew. Toto turned around to find Catface joining in with great gusto.

'Catface, what are you doing?' she asked, appalled.

'Just getting into character! Although I do like the sound of the riches. You can't deny it, he's a charming fellow don't you think?'

Toto shook her head in despair, then powered on towards her goal.

'Now that we've set sail, I shall divulge my plan,' Archduke Ferdicat continued, the sailors hanging on every word. 'For years, we've had to watch from the armchairs and the laps of those idiot humans while they made mistake after mistake. Global warming, wars ... not to mention the declining standards of furniture produced for cat napping, and what passes for cat food nowadays ...'

The crowd murmured in agreement.

'The only way for things to change is to take back control and for cats – the most intelligent species of all – to run the world. And that starts here, *TONIGHT!*'

A loud cheer came up from the deck.

'I have to be honest, he talks a terrific game. Are you *SURE* he's the *BADDIE?*' whispered Silver jokingly to his sister.

'Yes, together we will make the world a better place.'

A cheer went up, but not as loud as the last one.

'A world where cats have the power but also a lot of responsibility.'

The next cheer was the weakest yet.

'Oh, for kitty's sake,' the Archduke said under his breath.

'And yes, where you are all rich and don't need to work ever again.'

The cheer went through the roof.

'Tonight, we hit the humans and the traitorous animals who support them where it hurts: **WE HAVE THEIR CHEESE!** Without it they are powerless and will turn on each other.'

'We will hold the cheese ransom in the Artic until those idiots, the Ancient Order of International Ninja Cats agrees to our terms. Oh, they can have their precious cheese back (minus your shares, of course) with one little addition: a gift. Every human world leader must accept a small, vulnerable, abandoned, **CUTE** cat. Look at them, with their I'm-so-adorable faces!'

He gestured to his right where there were fifty or so kittens who looked exactly like him.

'After all, what human can resist a fluffy kitten? And what respectable ninja would turn an abandoned kitty away? Their ridiculous code of honour means they'll have to take them in! But these are no ordinary kittens. Meet my children, nephews, nieces, and a couple of third cousins three times removed – all trained Ferdicats and all ready to carry out my bidding.'

The Archduke let out what was meant to be a menacing laugh. It was the weirdest high pitched screechy meow the cats had ever heard. **'MMMEEEOOOWWWHAHAHA!'**

All the cats on deck put their paws in their ears, but he didn't seem to notice.

'In no time I will put an end to those pesky ninja cats!'

He let out the terrible laugh again, **'MMMEEEOOOWWWHAHAHA!'**

And swished his cape importantly.

'Curses, it's one of those "Evil Genius Plans",' whispered Toto to the others. 'I learned all about those from my sensei, Ventura, they are the worst! We have to **STOP** him!'

'What can we do? We can't fight all of them … even with our ninja powers.' said Silver.

'**MY** ninja powers,' Toto answered. 'Look, as far as I can see, the only power the Archduke has is that he has possession of the cheese. So, let's stick to the plan. Come on, we're nearly there.'

Slowly, they snuck up the steps which led to the upper deck and the wheelhouse. They were going to pass right by the Archduke, but luckily he was still in full flow.

'So, I say to you, stick with your Archduke, the Big D, the Dukemeister, and together cats will rule the world once and for all!'

The deck below turned instantly into pandemonium, hats were being waved, there were howls and meows, rats were getting tossed in the air in celebration.

Then, suddenly, the Archduke spotted the trio out of the corner of his eye.

'WHO ARE YOU? WHY AREN'T YOU IN RAPTURES LISTENING TO ME? AND WHERE DO YOU THINK YOU ARE GOING?'

Elias Copinger piped up. 'Hang on a minute, boss. I know these two. Larry sent them – they were in the Sour Saucer. This is Christopher,' he said gesturing to Silver, 'and this is his sister, Columbus.'

'I know he's very intimidating and all that, but he's really not that bright, is he?' Toto said to Silver.

'AND THIS,' Elias said, making a lunge for Catface and grabbing him by the shirt, 'is the guy who came to their rescue. Boy, am I looking forward to getting my claws into you.'

'Spies? Interfering little ninjas?' the Archduke said very matter of factly. 'Oh well, they can't be allowed to get in the way of our mission ... throw them overboard.'

And with that, he swished his cape once more and made for the wheelhouse.

'With pleasure, boss,' the menacing cat snarled as he hoisted Catface towards the edge of the boat. His fellow goons closed in on Toto and Silver.

'Toto, now might be an idea for that excellent training of yours to kick in,' squeaked Catface.

The storm clouds closed in. But in the dim moonlight Toto could still make out the shadows looming towards her and Silver.

'Sis, I've had an idea. You handle these chaps, and I'll sort the rest of the crew,' her brother whispered.

'Silver, you can't ... there are hundreds of sailors down there. You don't stand a chance— Silver?'

But it was too late, her brother was gone. Whatever he had planned he was going to be on his own.

Toto turned to confront the four henchcats now almost upon her.

Emptying her mind, she drew breath and concentrated, but the ship was rocking from side to side, and it was difficult to hold steady.

Suddenly, one of the Siamese cats leapt at her with a **FLYING KICK**, which could have been deadly if not for the huge wave which suddenly crashed into the boat, making the Siamese lose her footing at the last minute. Toto dodged to one side, grabbed hold of the bigger cat's leg, swung her around and sent her flying into her pal. They tumbled overboard and crashed into the sea below.

'HEEELLPPP!' they cried. They might have been her enemies, but Toto couldn't bear the thought of the cats in the water. She could make out the shape of a life raft on the side of the boat and she quickly loosened it.

'*THAAAANK YOOOOU!*' Toto heard as she turned to face the last of her foes.

Behind them she could just about make out Catface, now dangling in mid-air over the dark ocean in Elias's vice-like grip. She had to move fast.

She took a run at the final two cats and just as they were about to both throw a punch she threw herself into a slide on the wet deck, arching her back so she ducked between them. By the time they'd worked out what she was doing it was too late; their punches connected and they knocked each other out cold.

Toto came out of her slide right next to Elias and Catface.

'Too late, little ninja! I hope you can swim, both of you!' Elias laughed as he let go of Catface, who went tumbling through the sea air into the darkness.

'Arrrrgghhh, I'm too young and far too good-looking to die!' screamed the rat as he plunged towards the sea.

Toto's instincts took over. Before she knew it, she'd picked up a rope attached to the rail of the ship and, taking a running jump, dived overboard to save her friend.

She caught up with Catface barely a few centimetres from the sea.

Toto used their momentum to swing them both back on deck, where Elias was watching in disbelief. Before he had time to act, she tied the rope tightly around him, and lashed it to the rail.

'What the—? Why you little—! Ouch, this really chaffs! Does it have to be this tight?'

Catface ran over to Toto and lifted her off her feet in an almighty hug. 'That was genius!'

'Thanks, Catface, but we're not safe yet ... we've got a job to do! We need to deal with the rest of the crew and then track down the Archduke.'

'Well I don't think the crew will be much of a problem,' answered Catface, 'check Silver out!'

Silver was at the other end of the deck. He'd opened the enormous hatch that led directly down to the hold and was calling to the crew with a small loudspeaker.

'Get your tuna, lovely canned tuna, all in beautiful olive oil. Can openers available. Get your ration of tuna for the days ahead, top quality sourced by me, the err, the catering officer.'

'All right!' one of the ship's crew cheered.

'Let's eat!' said another.

In no time, the whole hungry crowd had jostled their way below deck towards the canned goodies, leaving Silver to close the hatch and lock it tight to trap the crew in the bowels of the ship.

'Amazing plan!' Toto said to her brother as he proudly strutted over.

'I just thought with my belly,' he replied. 'I knew that would work one day!'

'OK, there's not a moment to lose. Catface,

get to the bridge and turn this ship around'

'Where are you going?' he asked, concerned.

'To find Archduke Ferdicat.'

The wind was starting to howl, and the waves were getting bigger. In the distance they heard the **RUMBLING OF THUNDER**. An angry storm was fast approaching.

Catface shook his head. 'Are you crazy? He's finished, all his gang are captured, or beaten, or eating! Let's just get this cheese home.'

'No, we can't let him get away with—'

'Sis, he's on top of the wheelhouse!' Silver cried.

Toto strained her eyes. She could just about see the moon light up a shadowy figure above them. She felt certain he'd seen the whole thing play out and she could sense his eyes were bearing down on her. He stood stock still for a few seconds and then with a dramatic twirl of his cape he was gone.

WHOOOOSH

CHAPTER 10

'There's nowhere for him to run to,' shouted Silver. The thunder storm was raging around the cats as they ran towards the stern of the boat in pursuit of the Archduke.

'Don't underestimate him; this guy is one of the greatest ninjas ever,' Toto yelled back.

'Then what chance do we have? You've only just graduated and I ... well, I'm not even a ninja!'

'We've got to do something. If he gets

away then he'll just come back with another evil plan.'

Although Toto relied on her brother for his sight, with the lightning illuminating the sky, she could just about make out the shapes of the seemingly endless line of barges being towed behind the ship. Beyond, the coastline was disappearing fast.

'Where is he?' said Toto.

Silver trained his eyes against the rain and whooped, 'he's trying to get to the end of the line of barges – I can see his black cape flapping in the wind!'

Toto acted on pure *INSTINCT*. Effortlessly, she jumped over the rails onto the first barge, then began sprinting over the mounds of cheese after the Archduke.

'Show off,' Silver smiled to himself, and took off in a not-so-high-speed chase after the ninjas. Unfortunately, his first leap landed him straight into a barge full of gooey ricotta.

'Oh blast, it'll take me ages to get out
here ... but it is rather **TASTY** ...' said Silver
as he began to eat himself free.

The barges were being tossed about by
the waves so violently that Toto and the

Archduke were struggling the stay upright.
But Toto was smaller and more agile, and
she was gaining on the master ninja.

'Give up,' she cried. 'We've captured all
your gang, and there's nowhere left to run
to – it's hopeless.'

'Quite the contrary, my little teacher's
pet, I merely have to get rid of you, and the
advantage swings in my favour once again,
MMMEEEOOOWWWHAHAHA!'

That laugh is so annoying, Toto thought
to herself, as she stepped up her pursuit.

By now they had reached the second-to-last barge (full to the brim of bouncy mozzarella). The older cat turned and drew his sword. As he did so, the ship slowly began to turn back to shore.

'Catface, you've done it!' Toto whispered gleefully. His success filled her with more confidence for the fight ahead.

The cats began to circle each other, as the rain and wind swirled about them.

'It's a pity, my little ninja, that you are so obedient to your master Larry. You would have been a very useful ally in my quest to create a world where cats reign supreme.'

'No,' replied Toto, 'Silver and I like the world as it is. The humans aren't perfect, (and I believe it's a scientific fact that they have smaller brains than us), but they love us. We've all got to respect each other, no matter where we come from and what species we belong to. So, come on, put down the sword, and let's talk this through.'

The Archduke rolled his eyes. 'Argh, how boring – are you finished? I could just hear Larry and Ventura spilling out of your mouth. What a load of old **NONSENSE**. Now, any last words?'

Toto looked stunned.

'No? Then can I please get on with defeating you and getting my mission back on track?' At this, he drew his sword ready for battle.

'I would try and make it quick,' he said, 'but to play with my prey is so much more fun.'

He thrust his rapier right at Toto, who only just swivelled out of the way in time.

The Archduke lunged again and this time she wasn't as lucky. As she dived out of the way, the blade caught her side and grazed her.

'Oww,' she yelled.

SWOOSH

'Oh, stop moaning, that's just a scratch, plenty more where that came from ...'

Again and again he came for her, his footwork and technique were exquisite. On dry land it would have been hard enough for Toto to evade his blows, but with the barges rolling around in the crashing waves, it was *IMPOSSIBLE*. Toto started to tire – without a weapon of her own she simply didn't have an answer to the superior warrior. Finally, he kicked her feet from underneath her and she collapsed on her back, breathing heavily.

'What a waste ... Goodbye, Toto,' the Archduke said, lifting the sword above his head ready to strike her.

Toto shut her eyes and put her paws in front of her face to await the blow that was

to surely come—

'What? How? **NOOOO** ...'

She opened her eyes to see the sword only

millimetres from her face. Instinctively, she had unsheathed her claws for protection and somehow caught the blade between them. As she looked up at the bigger cat she could sense his hesitation and panic. She knew this was her chance.

'**PURRS, PAWS AND CLAWS**,' she whispered to herself.

Summoning her fading strength, she brought all four paws to her chest, then with kicked for her life, sending the Archduke sailing into the night air.

'**AARRGGHH!**' he yelled as he landed bottom first on the last barge of the convoy and went straight through the tarpaulin

into mounds of ripe, smelly (delicious) Camembert.

Toto, finding newfound strength, got straight to her feet. But before she could leap to the final barge to capture the Archduke once and for all, a huge wave crashed against it and broke the rope that attached it to the rest of the convoy. The mountain of camembert and Archduke Ferdicat drifted off into the rolling sea.

Toto put her face in her paws. She couldn't believe he'd escaped her grasp. Now he'd be free to plot a new **EVIL GENIUS PLAN**.

In the distance, the Archduke's wails could just about be heard over the wind. 'Argh ... I'm all smelly ... It's going to take ages to get this out in the wash ... my lovely cape ... my suit ... and there's cheese all over my sword ... I'll get you for this, I swear, you little **PIPSQUEEEEAK** ...'

When Toto could no longer make out the fuzzy outline of the Camembert, she turned and could sense the lights of land getting closer. Her brother and her friend stood on the bridge of the boat waving to her and beaming with pride.

*

Larry looked delighted as he greeted Toto and the team at the dockside. 'Well done, Toto – almost all of the cheese recovered! Though it's a shame about the Camembert – that's my favourite. Shelia has alerted the human authorities who'll be around to pick it up very soon. The Archduke and a whole army of ruffians thwarted, eh? Not bad for your first mission.'

Catface had successfully moored The Flyin' Fish, and the animal police force was frog marching the Archduke's gang down the gang planks and into custody.

'Toto, I have to tell you, Ferdicat won't take kindly to this humiliation. He'll be back and he'll be gunning for all of us.'

'We'll be ready for him,' said Silver,

'right, sis?'

'You heard him, boss, ready with **PURRS, PAWS AND CLAWS**' beamed Toto.

'What a perfectly brilliant trio you are,' said Larry with a smile.

'I say, do you fancy coming back to Number 10? We've got cheese to eat, and a mission to celebrate. I've even got some special gold top milk in the fridge.'

Silver looked at Toto eagerly, but she was busy yawning an almighty yawn.

'I think it might be time to get these two to bed,' said Catface. He called out into the sky, again in awful seagull. Three familiar shapes began to appear. The team saluted Larry then boarded the gulls who circled the scene below before turning west to fly them home.

'That is quite a sight.'

Catface gazed down at the big ship, the scores of barges full of cheese moored up behind it, and the blue lights of the human police cars snaking their way towards the scene.

But the kittens weren't listening to him, they'd fallen fast asleep the minute they'd taken off, nestled in the warm feathers of the seagulls.

It was gone dawn by the time Toto and Silver clambered through their cat flap, desperate to fall into their baskets for a proper cat nap.

'And where do you two think you've been all night?' Mamma asked.

'Been out raving in Camden Town, I bet!' Papa laughed, then he added, 'hey, if you play your cards right, you might get a bit of our dinner this evening. I hear the cheese shop is back open, so I'm doing your favourite: **MACARONI CHEESE!**'

The cats looked at each other and ran straight up the stairs to bed.

'Fussy little things, no pleasing some cats,' Mamma said, shaking her head.

EPILOGUE

It was a windy morning in the French coastal town of Deauville and the mayor, Monsieur Jean-Paul Rochebuet, was not a happy man.

Only a few miles down the road was the town of Camembert, but the local delicious cheese was nowhere to be found. They'd run out and had no idea where the cheese had gone or when it would be back. People

were getting restless and grumpy, and it was causing all sorts of damage to the mayor's reputation.

He was taking a walk down on the beach to clear his head. **REALLY, NO CAMEMBERT?** It was a disaster that could cost him his job. Up ahead, he saw a large, unusual shape – was it a marooned boat? Even though he was busy and in the depths of despair, he'd have to go and investigate and let the coastguard know.

As he got closer, he could smell a familiar **WHIFF** of something that made his heart soar … It couldn't be, could it? It was! He pulled back the tarpaulin to reveal a mountain of Camembert and on top of it, a beautiful cat who seemed to be wearing a small cape, and was covered in cheese.

'Monsieur Chat! Merci, merci! Come here, and let me give you a **CUDDLE!** Sacré bleu!'

'I'll get you for this Toto, mark my words,' Ferdicat muttered to himself. 'As soon as I've dry-cleaned this cape, then you are mine. Oh, I hate humans ... but I have to say this Mayor does give a good cuddle ... hmm, maybe I'll stay a while and see what I can do in this town ... *MEEEOOOWWWHAHAHA* ...'

THE END

HAVE YOU READ TOTO'S FIRST ADVENTURE?

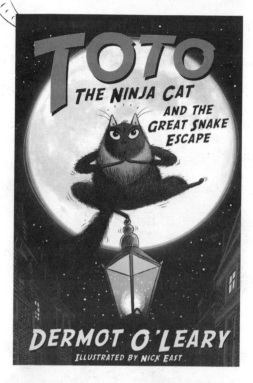

A deadly king cobra has escaped from London Zoo, and Toto's going to have to use all her powers to capture him ...

NOW AVAILABLE AS AN AUDIO BOOK, TOO!

ACKNOWLEDGEMENTS

Firstly, and most importantly, thanks so much to the stars of the show Toto, and Silver. Thanks for being excellent and cuddly housemates (anyone who tells you cats aren't affectionate ... well, just doesn't know cats!). We love that you non-verbally fill us in on your night-time adventures when you come in and tread on our heads at five in the morning. Although we wish we could rely on you to help around the house (cats are shocking at stacking the dishwasher).

While we're thanking our feline friends ... a big hello to the newest member of the O'Leary/Koppang household: Socks, aka Crazy Pants/Crazy town/Captain Crazy, who is exactly what he says on the tin. Thanks for the morning squeaky smooches. I'm looking forward to seeing what your adventures hold. Now, please stop biting my face.

Thanks to Jane, Rachel, Carly, and all at Battersea Dogs and Cats Home who looked after Socks when he was inexplicably given up for adoption. If you're reading this and thinking about getting a cat or a dog, there are thousands of furry friends out there in need of loving homes at Battersea, the Dogs Trust, Celia Hammond, the RSPCA, and countless other excellent organisations and charities across the UK.

Eternal gratitude to all the team at Hachette, especially the wise, and frankly presidential, Anne McNeil (McNeil for PM!!), the tiggerishly enthusiastic, cup-half-full merchant, Alison Padley and all those teams who work tirelessly behind the scenes to get Toto onto shelves around the world. Huzzah for the smiling, graceful, wisdom of Kate Agar, plus a notable mention in dispatches for Sarah Lambert, whose guidance on the first Toto book will be never be underestimated or forgotten.

As always, there's no way Toto would have come to life without the brilliant work of Nick East. Nick, thank you for making the pages come alive. I'm (almost) glad that the part of my brain drawing is filed under finished maturing when I got to three years old, so that I get to see the incredible and inspiring art you always produce.

Thanks to the team at the finest management company a broadcaster could ask for: John, Jonny and Jess at John Noel Management. It's invaluable to work with a great team, and you are family.

Thanks also to the glam, swishy, sassy smarty squad of Liz, Jordan and all at Liz Matthews PR, and also to the force of nature that is Fritha Lindqvist (excellent spy name, by the way) who somehow, somehow always arrives before me, and never without at least two enormous bags of books in tow.

To Polly and Sarah for always keeping the pot boiling and the diary nothing less than Swiss.

Thanks, of course, to all at The Village Vets, especially Fran, for the compassion and care with which they treat all animals.

Thanks to my Mam and Dad for lighting the reading fire early and keeping it stoked.

A quick thanks to L. A. Vocelle, whose book Revered and Reviled: A Complete History of the Domestic Cat was incredibly useful.

And finally, thanks to my wife Dee for being the best God darn partner an Italian-Ninja-Cat-writing author could wish for. These books, of which I am very proud, would be a shadow of what they are without your counsel, your humour, your quirks and your smarts.

DERMOT O'LEARY'S

television and radio work has made
him a household name.

Dermot started his career on T4 for Channel 4, and has
presented shows for both ITV and the BBC.
His best-known work includes ten series of The X Factor,
Big Brother's Little Brother, BBC3's First Time Voters
Question Time, Unicef's Soccer Aid, the RTS Award
winning 'Live from Space' season following
the International Space Station's orbit of the Earth in 2014
and the Brit Awards which he presented with
Emma Willis in 2016.

2017 saw Dermot launch his new Saturday morning show
on BBC Radio 2, 'Saturday Breakfast with Dermot O'Leary'.
Previously in the Saturday afternoon slot, 'The Dermot
O'Leary Show' won three Sony Radio Awards and was well
known for its support of new and emerging bands.

2018 saw Dermot host the National Television Awards
for the ninth time. He also joined Kirsty Young and Huw
Edwards to host the BBC's coverage of the Royal Wedding
in front of an audience of 13 million people.

Toto the Ninja Cat and the Incredible Cheese Heist is
Dermot's second children's book. He lives in London with
his wife Dee and their cats Socks and, of course, Toto.